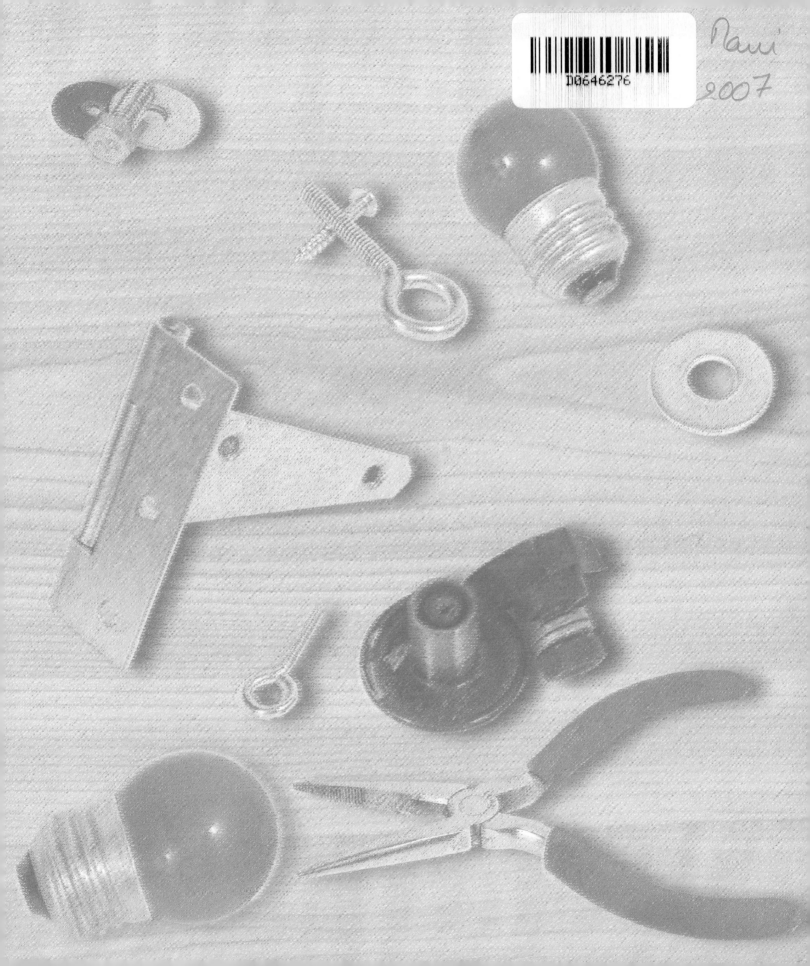

Naui
2007

ISLAND HERITAGE™
P U B L I S H I N G
A DIVISION OF THE MADDEN CORPORATION

94-411 Kōʻaki Street, Waipahu, Hawaiʻi 96797
Orders: (800) 468-2800
Information: (808) 564-8800
Fax: (808) 564-8877
islandheritage.com

ISBN NO. 0-93154-868-3
First Edition, First Printing - 2004

Mr. Miyataki's Marvelous MACHINE

Written by **Tandy Newsome**
Illustrated by **Don Robinson**

ISLAND HERITAGE™
PUBLISHING

Mr. Miyataki peered at his wrinkled reflection in the mirror and adjusted his red silk bow tie. He pushed his thick, black-framed glasses back onto his nose, and combed his neatly trimmed gray hair.

His grandson Sean watched excitedly.

"This is your very last day at the sushi factory, Grandpa," Sean said. "What are you going to do every day when you don't have to go to work?"

Lost in thought, Mr. Miyataki didn't answer. Instead, he slipped on his jacket and motioned to Sean to come along.

"We have a party to attend," he replied rather glumly.

They arrived at the gray factory with its faded red trim and were greeted by a large group of people.

"Hooray for Miyataki-san!" the crowd of workers cheered as they gathered around the small, elderly man.

"Arigato, arigato," he thanked them, bowing humbly. He was not used to so much attention. His small wooden desk was stacked with brightly wrapped gifts. He had worked at the factory since he was a young man, and he really didn't want to retire. He liked waking up to the sunrise, doing his exercises, and eating his fish and rice before walking four blocks to his job. He liked hearing the whirring sound of the machines as the sushi was packed in its distinctive, cellophane wrappers. He liked the busy feeling when everyone was working and the sense of pride he felt when customers said that their sushi was *"the best you could get anywhere."* And most of all, he liked the days when groups of schoolchildren came in long, yellow buses to see how the sushi was made. But Mr. Miyataki was sixty-five years old, and the rules of the factory stated that it was time for him to retire.

"You'll have time to plant a big garden now," said Mr. Tanabe enviously.

"We can go fishing and camping, and I'll teach you to play video games!" Sean added.

"You can just sleep all day if you want to!" shouted Joe, the janitor, who really didn't care much for work and slept every chance he got. Everyone laughed. Mr. Miyataki laughed too, but he did not know what he would do. He went to bed that night not sure if he was happy or sad.

The next morning, he was up by five o'clock as usual, for old habits are hard to break. He exercised, ate his breakfast, and decided to call on Mr. Kimura, an old friend. Mr. Kimura was sleeping in a rocking chair on his *lānai* when Mr. Miyataki arrived.

"Wake up Kimura-san! I am retired from my job now. Let's go fishing!" he announced excitedly. He remembered their early morning fishing trips.

"Oh, I don't think so, dear old friend," Mr. Kimura answered wearily. "My arms and legs are not strong like they used to be. My doctor says I am too weak for fishing."

Disappointed, Mr. Miyataki went fishing by himself. The next day he decided to visit Mrs. Morita. She was watching the cars going up and down her street.

"Aloha, Mrs. Morita," he said. "Remember me? How's your garden growing these days? I was wondering if you'd like to go to the orchid show with me this afternoon."

"Well, well, Mr. Miyataki!" she said. "It's nice to see you again, but my hands are too stiff for gardening now and my eyes have trouble seeing the flowers. Thank you, but I don't think I can go."

Mr. Miyataki glanced at her garden, completely overgrown with weeds. Reluctantly, he went to the orchid show by himself.

Not one to give up, the next morning he went to see one more of his old friends, Mr. Tanaka. He was encouraged to find him walking around his yard looking at his fruit trees.

"Good morning, Mr. Tanaka. It's been a long time," said Mr. Miyataki hopefully. "How about a lively game of cards? Remember how we used to play late into the night?"

"I'd love to, old friend, but my memory is slow now. I cannot remember how to play the game," Mr. Tanaka replied sadly.

Mr. Miyataki stayed a while longer, and then went home. Seeing his friends had made him feel old and tired, too, and he collapsed into his favorite chair. That afternoon after school, Sean stopped by to see him.

Mr. Miyataki was slumped in his chair and the boy noticed immediately that his grandfather was not feeling well.

"What's the matter, Grandpa? Why do you look so sad?" Sean asked softly.

"I guess this is how folks feel when they're too old to work like me," the little man replied, remembering Mr. Kimura's weak legs, Mrs. Morita's stiff hands, and Mr. Tanaka's slow memory. Sean had never heard him sound like this before.

"Grandpa, tell me about when you were young!" Sean said suddenly. He knew that his grandpa loved to tell him stories about when he was young.

"I was a lot like you, Sean," the old man began, reaching for a large black album from the stack of books by his chair. He turned the pages slowly. Each one contained snapshots of important moments in his life. A small clipping fell from between the pages. Sean picked up the yellowed piece of newsprint and unfolded it carefully. It was a photograph of a young boy not much older than himself, and he was standing next to a huge machine he had made.

"Is that you, Grandpa?" Sean asked excitedly.

Mr. Miyataki gazed at himself in the picture. The caption beneath the photo told of an award-winning science project he had built. The old man smiled to himself and closed his eyes for a moment, remembering that day long ago. He had been so proud when people had gathered around to ask him questions about his creation.

Suddenly, Sean shot up out of his seat.

"Let's build something, Grandpa! Let's build something marvelous!"

Mr. Miyataki turned to look at Sean, a sparkle growing in his old eyes. He had always loved tinkering with mechanical things and had dreamed of inventing something important one day, but the job at the sushi factory had come along and he had forgotten all about his dream. He thought about his friends who felt too old and tired to do things, and suddenly had an extraordinary idea. His fatigue vanished and he leaped out of his chair excitedly.

"Yes, we will build something, Sean. And it will be marvelous!" he said.

Sean couldn't wait.

"How will it work? What will we use? When can we start?" he asked. Sean had a million questions and could not sit still. His grandpa was mumbling something as he hurried to his desk and began sketching on a piece of paper.

Over the next few weeks the two of them were always together. They gathered spare parts from everywhere—the junkyard, secondhand stores, and even the city dump! Mr. Miyataki then went to visit his friends again.

"I'm beginning a project of great importance, and I desperately need your help!" he told them. He left each of them wondering what the project was and how they could possibly help.

He chose a spot in the center of his front yard and began working day and night. His neighbors heard hammering, sawing, and buzzing noises at all hours of the day. Traffic stalled in front of his house as people stopped to see what was going on. Everyone was talking about the steady flurry of activity.

And everyone who saw it marveled at the machine. There were knotted ropes and slippery slides, colorful pulleys and spinning wheels, steps, ladders, whistles and fans, and all were connected and moving together like an enormous mechanical spider.

News of the unusual project spread quickly and soon folks came from near and far to see what all the fuss was about. Some brought wood, nails, and cans of paint. Some came with picnic lunches and coolers of cold drinks. Others brought guitars and 'ukulele. Everyone worked together, old friends and new ones, young and old alike, and the incredible machine continued to grow bigger and more interesting each day. Sean made a sign that hung on the fence. It read, *"Mr. Miyataki's Marvelous Machine."*

One day Mr. Miyataki noticed his friend Mr. Kimura leaning on the fence watching all of the bustle and clatter.

"What does your contraption do, Miyataki?" he wanted to know, as he watched folks measuring, hammering, and painting.

"You'll find out soon enough. Why don't you give us a hand?" Mr. Miyataki said. Mr. Kimura was suddenly quite curious and he grabbed a hammer and some nails.

A week later Sean noticed Mr. Kimura's cane lying on a pile of wood scraps. Mrs. Morita's daughter brought her over so she could see what all the commotion was about, and soon Mrs. Morita couldn't resist planting flowers around the edge of the ever-expanding machine. A few days later, even Mr. Tanaka was perched high on a ladder with a paintbrush in his hand.

"This reminds me of when I was a boy climbing all over the monkey bars in the schoolyard," he said joyfully. "I didn't think I could do this anymore!"

Mr. Miyataki smiled. He wondered if Mr. Tanaka remembered how to play cards now, too.

23

One day Sean noticed something. "Grandpa, Mrs. Morita hasn't been here at all this week and I haven't seen Mr. Kimura either. I wonder where they are?"

"Well Sean, Mrs. Morita has begun taking care of her neglected garden again, and Mr. Tanaka has organized a group of friends to play cards a few times a week. I think our machine is beginning to work," he said, with a wink and smile.

Sean thought for a moment. "I think we really did build something marvelous, Grandpa!"

25

The next day Mr. Kimura showed up with a fishing pole instead of a hammer.

"Miyataki-san! Let's go fishing!" he said. "Remember that place where we used to catch the big ones?"

Mr. Miyataki was so happy that he laughed out loud. "Sure I do, let's go."

Soon Mr. Miyataki and his friends no longer had time to work on the machine. Mr. Kimura opened a fishing shop in town. Mrs. Morita expanded her garden and began teaching gardening classes. And Mr. Tanaka began learning to do magic card tricks.

Mr. Miyataki goes fishing, works in his garden, plays cards, and sometimes even plays video games! And just like his days at the sushi factory, he enjoys watching groups of school children come in long yellow buses. But now they come to Mr. Miyataki's house to climb and play on his marvelous machine.

The End

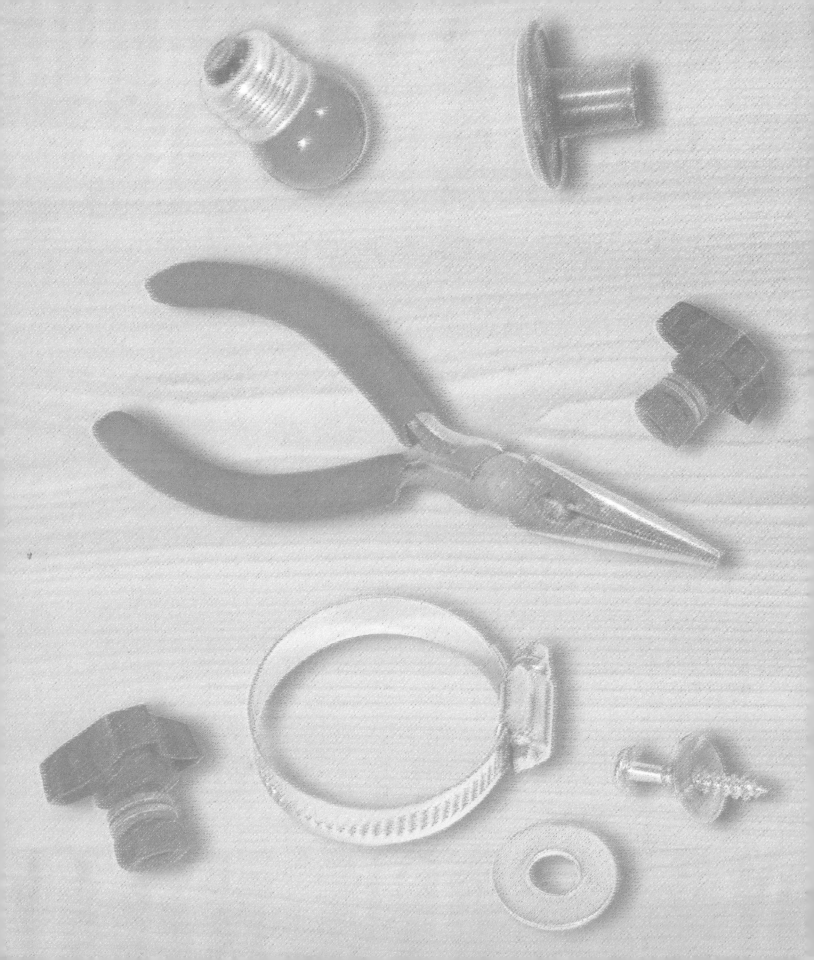